NICKELODEON

THE NAKED BROTHERS BAND

POSTER SONG BOOK

SCHOLASTIC INC.

New York Toronto London Auckland Sydney
Mexico City New Delhi Hong Kong Buenos Aires

Based on the television series *The Naked Brothers Band* created by Polly Draper

ISBN-13: 978-0-545-02072-7
ISBN-10: 0-545-02072-5

12 11 10 9 8 7 6 5 4 3 2 1   7 8 9 10 11 12/0

Interior designed by Two Red Shoes Design

Printed in the U.S.A.
First printing, November 2007

NICKELODEON
THE NAKED BROTHERS BAND

The Naked Brothers Band rocks the world and tops the charts! Formed by Nat and Alex Wolff, this rock group sounds sweeter than a banana smoothie, and has more hits than a hardcore wrestler! Their award-winning music videos, Nat's soulful vocals, and Alex's wild-man antics keep bringing the fans back for more.

NICKELODEON
THE NAKED BROTHERS BAND
NOT YOUR USUAL
ROCK STARS

Video cameras often follow the Wolff brothers, recording footage for their own TV show. Fans are able to see almost every aspect of their rock-star lives. Whether they're laying down tracks in the studio, making music videos, or trying to escape their dad's accordion, the cameras see it all—the good, the bad, and the silly!

Nickelodeon

The Naked Brothers Band

NAT

The Girl Magnet

NAME-NAT
BAND POSITION-LEAD VOCALS, KEYBOARD, SONGWRITER
NICKNAME-GIRL MAGNET

"CATCH UP WITH THE END"

No time for feelings
Or for love
Worship the man
On the bus stop
Brighten the day
Of a woman on the subway
Catch up with the end

Running like a chicken
Without its head
The universe is doing so
Rocking to bed
A baby that's not yours
Driving the Mustang
At full speed
Waiting for the
Same replica day
Catch up with the end

Don't do as I do
Won't you do as I say
I might make people angry
But that's a risk I'll take

Catch up with the end
Catch up with the end
Catch up with the end
Catch up with the end

Swimming in an ocean
Without water
Fell into a sack
Filled with quarters
Fighting the king
Of evolution
Dreaming of an
Imaginary land

Don't do as I do
Won't you do as I say
I might make people angry
But that's a risk I'll take

NICKELODEON
THE NAKED BROTHERS BAND
ALEX
WILD MAN

"That's How It Is"

Written by Alex Wolff

You like piano
I like drums
That's how it is
That's how it is

I have baby teeth
You have grown-up teeth
That's how it is
That's how it is

I play my Gameboy
You do homework
That's how it is
That's how it is

I wear a do-rag
You wear your hair
That's how it is
That's how it is

Name-Alex
Band Position-drummer, backup vocals
Favorite drink-milk

NICKELODEON
THE NAKED BROTHERS BAND
ROSALINA
ROCK 'N' ROLL
BABE

NAME-ROSALINA
BAND POSITION-BASS GUITAR, BACKUP VOCALS
FIRST TIME IN SPOTLIGHT- WHEN SHE APPEARED IN THE "CRAZY CAR" VIDEO

"GIRL OF MY DREAMS"

My mind turned around
I'm seeing things upside down
My mind turned around
I'm acting like a clown

'Cause the girl of my dreams
Was right next to me
And she was sitting on my lap

I didn't catch your name
But I'm going insane
I'm in love with the girl
I'm in love with a girl

I will find her
I will get her
I will make her
Little heart come through

I will see her
From miles away
From night to day
In my head

Oh oh oh oh
Oh oh oh oh oh
What if the girl of your dreams
Was right next to me

The girl of my dreams
Was right next to me
And she was sitting on my lap

I didn't catch your name
But I'm going insane
I'm in love with a girl

I will dream of her
When she's not there
When she is I will too

I will need her
As I do now
I will bow
For her affection

Ah ah ah
Ah ah ah ah ah
What if the girl
Of your dreams
Was right next to me?

The girl of my dreams
Was right next to me
And she was sitting on my lap

I didn't catch your name
But I'm going insane
I'm in love with the girl
I'm in love with the girl

NICKELODEON
THE NAKED BROTHERS BAND
QAASIM
SUPER GENIUS

"BANANA SMOOTHIE"

Cut up the bananas
Put it in a blender
And shake it all up
Shake it all up

You've got a banana smoothie
You've got a banana smoothie

Drink up, taste it, swallow it,
Get up, get on top of it
Feels right, aloha and mahalo

Cut up the bananas
Put it in a blender
And shake it all up
Shake it all up
You've got a banana smoothie
You've got a banana smoothie

Grow up, see it fading now
Rock out, leaving all of that
Feels right, aloha and mahalo

Die hard, furnace flying now
Rock out, leaving all of that
Feels right, aloha and mahalo

Cut up the bananas
Put it in a blender
And shake it all up
Shake it all up
You've got a banana smoothie
You've got a banana smoothie

Cut up the bananas
Put it in a blender
And shake it all up
Shake it all up

Cut up the bananas
Put it in a blender
And shake it all up
Shake it all up

NAME-QAASIM
BAND POSITION-LEAD GUITAR, BACKUP VOCALS
FULL NAME-QAASIM ASANI MALIK MIDDLETON

NICKELODEON
THE NAKED BROTHERS BAND

NICKELODEON
THE NAKED BROTHERS BAND
Brothers

THE NAKED BROTHERS BAND

NICKELODEON
THE NAKED BROTHERS BAND

NICKELODEON
THE NAKED BROTHERS BAND
DAVID
THE MAN WITH
THE MANNERS

NAME-DAVID
BAND POSITION-AUXILIARY KEYBOARD, BACKUP VOCALS
DOG'S NAME-E.T.

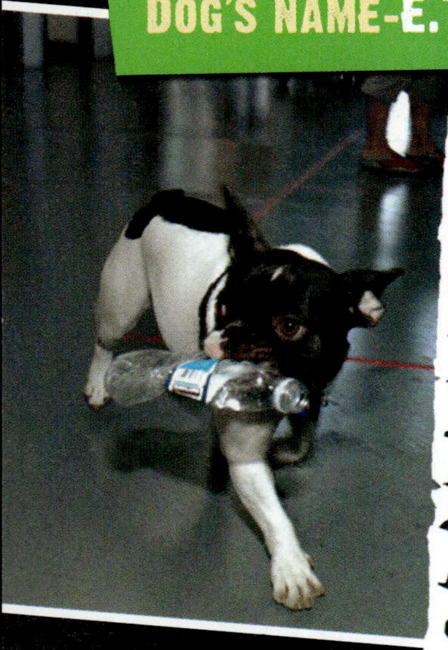

"SOMETIMES I'LL BE THERE"

I know of this place
I go some summer nights
It takes me up and down
Those shocking lights

It rocks me to bed
It doesn't know that I'm awake
Lady with a bowl of rice
A man turning off the light

Sometimes I'll be there
Sometimes I won't
Sometimes I'll see you there
Sometimes I won't
And I don't

'Cause it's my house
It's my day, it's my place
So go away
But you can stay
You can stay
You can stay
You can stay

The mysteries of the past
In one final blow
The future is the one that
must go
It's a table of conscience
In a room filled with tears
Chewed up sense of life
Drained from all these years

NICKELODEON
THE NAKED BROTHERS BAND
THOMAS
THE PRANKSTER

NAME-THOMAS
BAND POSITION-CELLO, BACKUP VOCALS
FAVORITE PASTIME-LIKES TO "TIE-DYE" HIS TONGUE WITH DIFFERENT FLAVORED POPSICLES

"L.A."

The time in our favorite place is going too fast
The time we spent here is already in the past

L.A. L.A. L.A. L.A. go today
L.A. L.A. L.A. L.A. it's a date
L.A. L.A. L.A. L.A. say hoorah

Sunshine happiness in Studio City

Pool out back
Yard out front
Happy dogs happy dogs

Universal Studios
In-N-Out
Sunset Boulevard
The big car wash hand

L.A. L.A. L.A. L.A. go today
L.A. L.A. L.A. L.A. it's a date
L.A. L.A. L.A. L.A. say hoorah

Sunshine happiness in Studio City

Movie stars in Hollywood
Staples Center
Sushi restaurant
And the yellow balloon

L.A. L.A. L.A. L.A. go today
L.A. L.A. L.A. L.A. it's a date
L.A. L.A. L.A. L.A. say hoorah

Sunshine City going around
Oh wow the flu is getting me down
How can you live in the rain or snow
When you can live in L.A.

L.A. L.A. L.A. L.A. go today
L.A. L.A. L.A. L.A. it's a date
L.A. L.A. L.A. L.A. say hoorah

L.A. L.A. makes your troubles go away
L.A. L.A. it's the day
L.A. L.A. why's everyone going away

Los Angeles
Los Angeles
Los Angeles
Los Angeles

NICKELODEON
THE NAKED BROTHERS BAND
COOPER
MANAGER
EXTRAORDINAIRE

NAME-COOPER
BAND POSITION-BAND MANAGER-PRODUCER-PROBLEM SOLVER
MOST COMMON ACCESSORY-CELL PHONE

"MOTOR MOUTH"

Bah-bah-bah-bah-bah
Bah-bah-bah-bah-bah
Bah-bah-bah-bah-bah
Bah-bah-bah-bah-bah

So you want to
I will save you
From the headache
That she gave you

With Motor Mouth
That's her name
Motor Mouth
She's insane

Chatter, chatter, chatter,
chatter box
Chatter, chatter, chatter,
chatter box

Bah-bah-bah-bah-bah
Bah-bah-bah-bah-bah
Bah-bah-bah-bah-bah
Bah-bah-bah-bah-bah

Here are the lyrics for two megahits the gang had back when they were The Silver Boulders!

"CRAZY CAR"

Crazy Car
To lead me nowhere
Lead me nowhere
Actually
It's made for that
Made for that

I have never seen you cry
But right now baby, why oh why
Take my hand and be my woman
Just for a day

Crazy Car
To lead me nowhere
Lead me nowhere
Actually
It's made for that
Made for that

Cra-ay-ay-ay-ay-ay-ay-zy Car
Cra-ay-ay-ay-ay-ay-ay-zy Car
Cra-ay-ay-ay-ay-ay-ay-zy Car
Cra-ay-ay-ay-ay-ay-ay-zy Car

Breaks my heart to see you sad
I have never felt this bad
Take my hand and be my woman
Just for a day

Crazy Car
To lead me nowhere
Lead me nowhere
Actually
It's made for that
Made for that

Cra-ay-ay-ay-ay-ay-ay-zy Car
Cra-ay-ay-ay-ay-ay-ay-zy Car
Cra-ay-ay-ay-ay-ay-ay-zy Car
Cra-ay-ay-ay-ay-ay-ay-zy Car

Cra-ay-ay-ay-ay-ay-ay-zy Car
Cra-ay-ay-ay-ay-ay-ay-zy Car
Cra-ay-ay-ay-ay-ay-ay-zy Car
Cra-ay-ay-ay-ay-ay-ay-zy Car

NICKELODEON
THE NAKED BROTHERS BAND
REAL BROTHERS
REAL MUSIC
NOT REALLY
NAKED

"IF THAT'S NOT LOVE"

If that's not love, then what is?
If that's not friendship, then what is?
If that's not music, then what is?

We've got that music in our blood
The magic ceases and then we're done
The magical feeling has begun
The magical feeling has begun

And before you know it we're there
On top of the world it seems
I don't know who or why or where
But I can still hear the music

If that's not love, then what is?
If that's not friendship, then what is?
If that's not music, then what is?

We've got that music in our blood
The magic ceases and then we're done
The magical feeling has begun
The magical feeling has begun

If that's not love, then what is?
If that's not friendship, then what is?
If that's not music, then what is?
If that's not music, then what is?
If that's not music, then what is?
If that's not music, then what is?

THE NAKED BROTHERS BAND
MOTOR IMPORTS
英国輸入

"I INDEED CAN SEE"

I indeed I indeed can see
I indeed I indeed can see

But the question is can you see me
But the question is can you see me

I indeed I indeed can see
I indeed I indeed can see

Everything will be alright
Everything will be OK

Just gotta hold on tightly
Just gotta stay with the group

I indeed I indeed can see
I indeed I indeed can see

But the question is can you see me
Yes the question is can you see me

I indeed I indeed can see
I indeed I indeed can see

"BEAUTIFUL EYES"

Blonde hair shiny blue eyes
Face made of gold
Hypnotized by the beautiful eyes
That draw me in

So please take my hand
I would be honored to dance with you
And maybe have a chance with you

Beautiful one beautiful girl
Hypnotized by your beautiful eyes

Beautiful eyes in disguise
It will arise
I despise any man who will
Take you away
Beautiful eyes

I'd be happy to sit with you
Tell you that life is all new
So please take my hand
Beautiful eyes in disguise

Beautiful eyes in disguise
It will arise
I despise any man who will
Take them away
Beautiful eyes

Beautiful eyes in disguise
It will arise
I despise any man who will
Take you away
Beautiful eyes

THE NAKED BROTHERS BAND
HARMONY

"NOWHERE"

I know this was supposed to be fun
I know all our troubles are done
But I don't feel right, I know we
were going to be alone
Together

I know we were going to be alone
Together

I miss my family
I miss my family
Not that you're not enough

But the road's so far
And we couldn't walk it
And we're in the middle
Of nowhere

I have mixed feelings right now
I know we've been planning this
For so long
I know we were going to be alone
Together

I miss my family
I miss my family
Not that you're not enough

But the road's so far
And we couldn't walk it
And we're in the middle of
Nowhere
And we're in the middle of
Nowhere

"I COULD BE"

I could be anything I wanna be
I could be anything I wanna be

Like a bird flying up in the tree
Like a bee stinging for honey

I could be anything I wanna be
I could be anything I wanna be

Like a fish swimming in the sea
Like a copy of someone like me

I could be
I could be
I could be
I could be

I could be anything I wanna be
I could be anything I wanna be

Like a skateboard prodigy

I could be anything I wanna be
I could be anything I wanna be

Like a frog jumping on a leaf
Like horses running free

I could be
I could be
I could be
I could be

NICKELODEON
THE NAKED BROTHERS BAND
ROCK ON

"I'M OUT"

If you're gonna treat me that way then I'm out
If you're gonna leave me that way then I'm out

'Cause I won't take your crying anymore
No I won't take your whining anymore

'Cause I'm out
I'm out
Oh, I'm out
I'm out
'Cause I won't take your crying anymore
No I won't take your whining anymore
'Cause I'm out
I'm out
Oh, I'm out
I'm out

If you're gonna treat me that way then I'm out
If you're gonna leave me that way then I'm out

'Cause I won't take your crying anymore
No I won't take your whining anymore
'Cause I'm out
I'm out
Oh, I'm out
I'm out
'Cause I'm out
I'm out
Oh, I'm out
I'm out